My Dad

To My Dad, my hero (with a new nose).

Love you lots!

Alfie

XX·

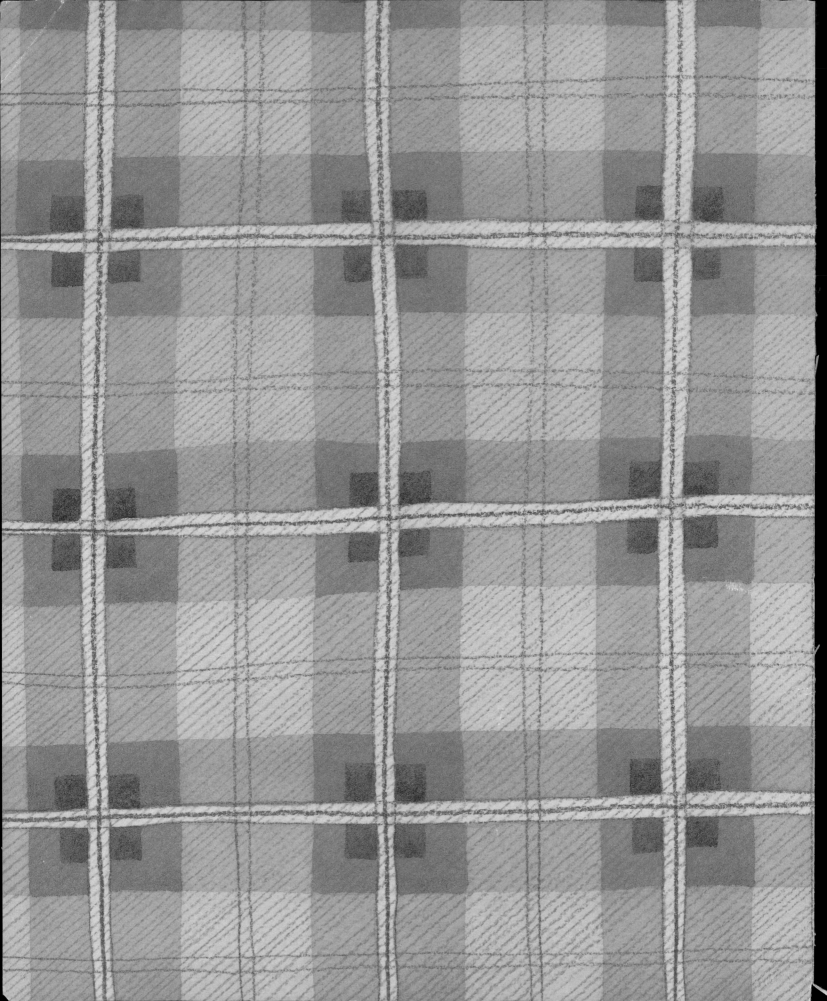

MY DAD
A PICTURE CORGI BOOK : 0552 546682

First published in Great Britain by Doubleday, a division of
Transworld Publishers

PRINTING HISTORY
Doubleday edition published 2000
Picture Corgi edition published 2001

1 3 5 7 9 10 8 6 4 2

Picture Corgi Books are published by Transworld Publishers,
61-63 Uxbridge Road, London W5 5SA,
a division of The Random House Group Ltd,
in Australia by Random House Australia (Pty) Ltd,
20 Alfred Street, Milsons Point, Sydney, NSW 2061,
in New Zealand by Random House New Zealand Ltd,
18 Poland Road, Glenfield, Auckland 10,
and in South Africa by Random House (Pty) Ltd,
Endulini, 5A Jubilee Road, Parktown 2193

Printed in Italy

My Dad

Anthony Browne

Picture Corgi

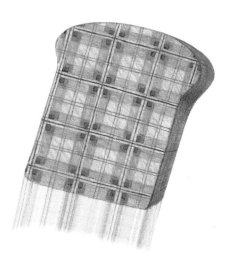

He's all right, my dad.

My dad isn't afraid of ANYTHING,

even the Big Bad Wolf.

He can jump right over the moon,

and walk on a tightrope (without falling off).

He can wrestle with giants,

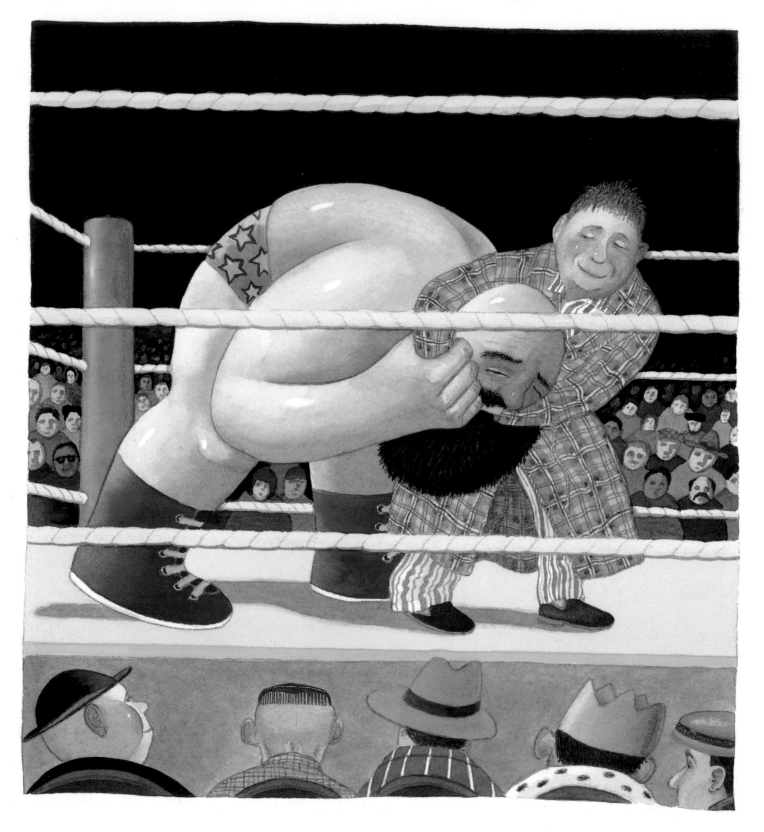

or win the fathers' race on sports day, easily.

He's all right, my dad.

My dad can eat like a horse,

and hc can swim like a fish.

He's as strong as a gorilla,

and as happy as a hippopotamus.

He's all right, my dad.

My dad's as big as a house,

and as soft as my teddy.

He's as wise as an owl,

and daft  as a brush.

He's all right, my dad.

My dad's a great dancer,

and a brilliant singer.

He's fantastic at football,

and he makes me laugh. A lot.

I love my dad.
And you know what?

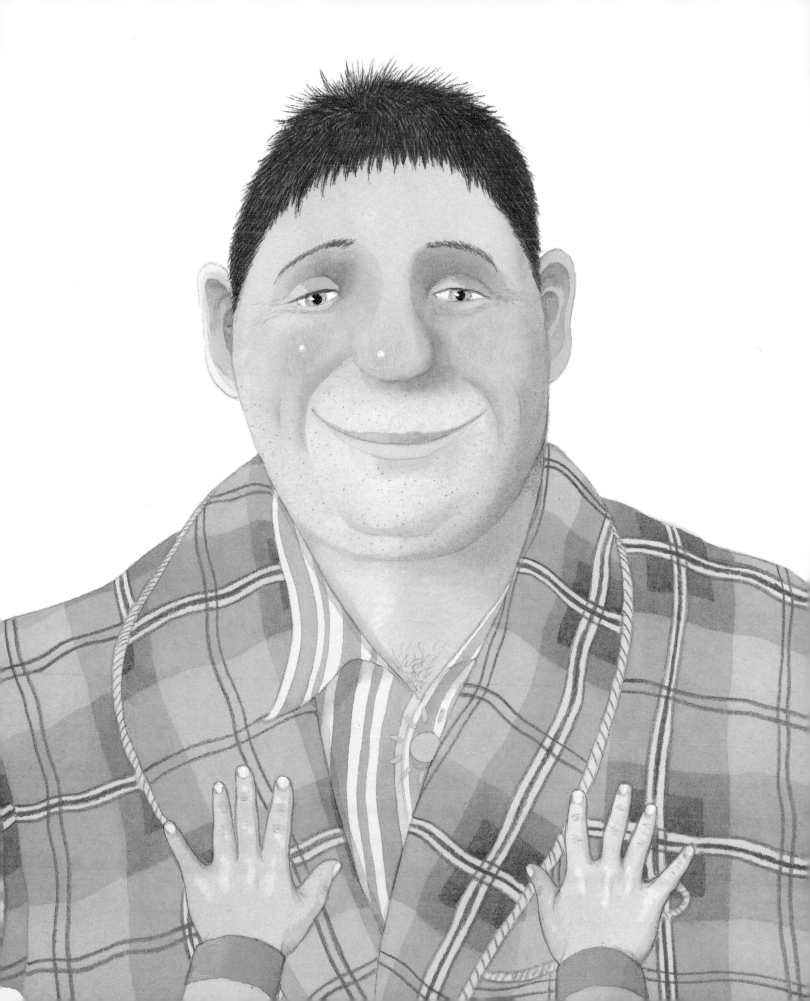

HE LOVES ME!

(And he always will.)

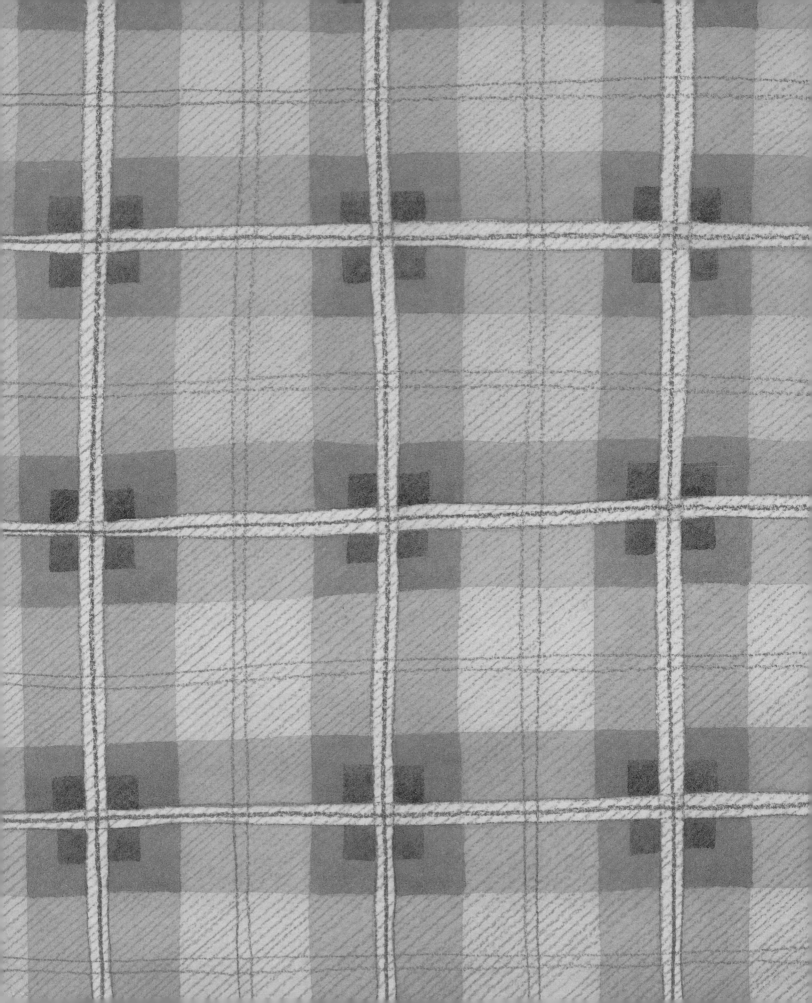

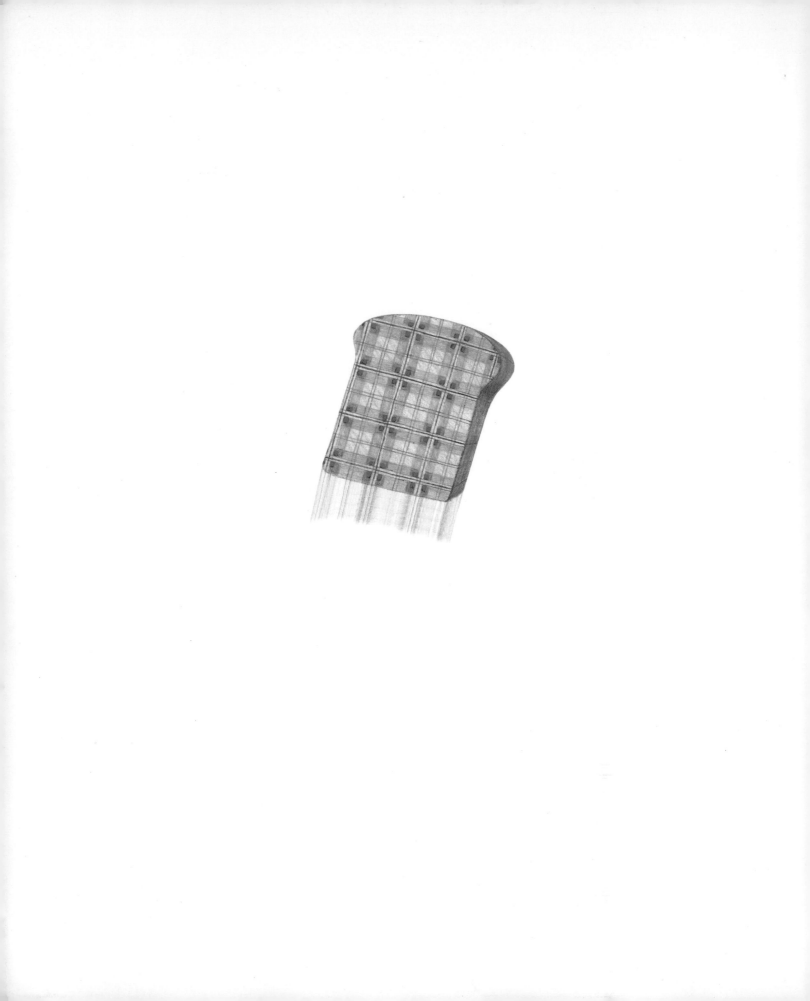